SILLY STORIES

TO TICKLE YOUR

FUNNY BONE

SeaStar Books

NEW YORK

Special thanks to Leigh Ann Jones, Valerie Lewis, Walter Mayes, and Marian Reiner for the consultation services and invaluable support they provided for the creation of this book.

Reading Rainbow® is a production of GPN/Nebraska ETV and WNED-TV Buffalo and is produced by Lancit Media Entertainment, Ltd., a JuniorNet Company. *Reading Rainbow*® is a registered trademark of GPN/WNED-TV.

 SeaStar Books · A division of North-South Books, Inc.

ISBN 1-58717-034-5 (library binding) 10 9 8 7 6 5 4 3 2 1
ISBN 1-58717-033-7 (paperback) 10 9 8 7 6 5 4 3 2 1

CONTENTS

PIZZA TIME

BY James Marshall

Fox saw his friend Dexter
coming out of the pizza parlor.
"You can't fire *me*," said Dexter.
"I quit!"
"Fine," said the boss.
"Maybe my next delivery boy
won't eat up all the pizza!"
Dexter left in a huff.
And Fox stepped inside
the pizza parlor.

"Do you have a job for me?" asked Fox.

"Do you like pizza?" said the boss.

"I prefer hot dogs," said Fox.

"Excellent," said the boss.

"Are you fast on your feet?"

"Like the wind," said Fox.

"Excellent," said the boss.

"Take this pizza over to Mrs. O'Hara.

She has been waiting a long time."

Fox was out the door in a flash.

On Homer's Hill
Fox picked up speed.
"I'm the fastest fox in town,"
he said.
At that moment
Louise came around the corner.
She was taking her pet mice
to the vet for their shots.

It was quite a crash!
Fox, Louise, and everything else
went flying.
They saw stars.

"Now you've done it!" said Fox.

"You've made me late.

I'll really have to step on it!"

And he hurried away.

Louise went to the vet's.

Doctor Jane opened the box.

"Where are your pet mice?" she said.

"This looks like a pizza."

"Uh-oh," said Louise.

Fox knocked on Mrs. O'Hara's door.
"It's about time," said Mrs. O'Hara.
"I'm having a party.
And we're just dying for pizza."
"It will be worth the wait," said Fox.

"Pizza time!"
said Mrs. O'Hara to her friends.
She opened the box.

Back at the pizza parlor
the boss was hopping mad.
"Mrs. O'Hara just called," he said.
"And you are fired!"
"Didn't she like the pizza?" said Fox.

THERE WAS A MAN DRESSED ALL IN CHEESE

BY Arnold Lobel

There was a man
Dressed all in cheese.
Certain was he
That the sight would please.
Though his neighbors agreed,
Those clothes looked well on him,
They ran far away
From that certain smell on him.

DRAGON SEES THE DAY

BY Dav Pilkey

One warm, sunny morning
Dragon woke up and yawned.
He was very groggy. . . .

And whenever Dragon woke up groggy,
he did *everything* wrong.
First, he read an egg
and fried the morning newspaper.

Then he buttered his tea
and sipped a cup of toast.

Finally Dragon opened the door
to see the day.
But Dragon did not see the sun.
He did not see the trees or the hills
or the flowers or the sky.
He saw only shadows.
"It must still be nighttime,"
said Dragon.

So he went back to bed.

HERE AND THERE

BY Nancy Jewell

PICTURES BY Lisa Thiesing

"Come here, Tuck,"
said Nip.

"I am here," called Tuck
from the other room.

"You are not here," called Nip.
"I want you to come here."

Tuck looked at his hands.
He looked at his feet.

He patted his belly
and pinched his cheek.

"But I *am* here," called Tuck.

"No," called Nip,
"only I am here."

Tuck looked to his right.
He looked to his left.
He looked up and down
and all around.
"I don't see you,"
called Tuck.

"You can't see me," called Nip.

"Why?" called Tuck.

"Because you are not here
to see me," called Nip.

"Can you see me?" Tuck called.

"No," called Nip,

"because you are not here!"

"But where am I?" called Tuck.

"You are There," called Nip.
"Where is There?" called Tuck.
"There is not Here!" called Nip.

"But where is Here?" called Tuck.
"Here is where I am," called Nip.

"How do I get to Here?" called Tuck.

"You come to where I am," called Nip.

So Tuck walked into the room
where Nip was.

"Now I am *here*," Tuck said.

"Yes," said Nip.

"Now we are both *here*."

"Why did you want me here?"
said Tuck.
"I forget," said Nip.

SEA HORSE AND SAWHORSE

BY X. J. Kennedy
PICTURE BY Henry Cole

A sea horse saw a sawhorse
On a seesaw meant for two.
"See here, sawhorse," said sea horse,
"May I seesaw with you?"
"I'll see, sea horse," said sawhorse.
"Right now I'm having fun
Seeing if I'll be seasick
On a seesaw meant for one."

A WIGGLY, JIGGLY, JOGGLY, TOOTH

BY Bill Hawley

PICTURES BY William Joyce

Kevin's tooth was loose.

He wiggled it with his tongue.

He jiggled it with his finger.

He wiggled and jiggled and joggled it.

His mother said, "Kevin, stop
wiggling that tooth."

His teacher said, "Kevin, stop
jiggling that tooth."

His friends said, "Kevin, stop
joggling that tooth."

Kevin didn't listen.
He wiggled and jiggled and
joggled it. And . . .

he swallowed it!

MY LITTLE BROTHER IS REALLY WEIRD!

BY Colin McNaughton

My little brother
Is really weird.
He's up and gone
And grown a beard!

Oh, the embarrassment,
Oh, the disgrace—
The neighbors call him
FUNGUS FACE!

WALLPAPER

BY Cynthia Rylant

PICTURES BY Mark Teague

Poppleton bought some wallpaper
for his kitchen.
He asked his friend Hudson
to help him hang it.

"Sure," said Hudson.
Hudson came over
on Saturday morning.

Poppleton and Hudson put some glue
on the back of the wallpaper.
Then they tried to hang it on the wall.
"Hold up your side, Hudson,"
said Poppleton.

"I *am* holding up my side,"
said Hudson.

Poppleton looked over at Hudson.

Hmmm, thought Poppleton.
Maybe I shouldn't have asked a
three-inch mouse to help hang wallpaper.
"I'll call Fillmore to help us,"
said Poppleton.

Fillmore came over to help.

"Hold up your part, Fillmore,"
said Poppleton.

Poppleton looked over at Fillmore.

Fillmore was chewing on the paper.

Hmmm, thought Poppleton.
Maybe I shouldn't have asked a goat
to help hang wallpaper.
"I'll call Cherry Sue to help us,"
said Poppleton.

Cherry Sue came over to help.

"Hold up your part, Cherry Sue,"

said Poppleton.

Poppleton looked over at Cherry Sue.

Cherry Sue was stuck to the glue.

Hmmm, thought Poppleton.
*Maybe I shouldn't have asked a llama
to help hang wallpaper.*

"How can I hang wallpaper," Poppleton complained to them all, "when Hudson is a mouse, and Fillmore is a goat, and Cherry Sue is a llama!"

The three friends looked at Poppleton.
"Oh dear," said Poppleton, ashamed.

"I can stand on a ladder," said Hudson.

"I can eat a big breakfast first,"
said Fillmore.

"I can get a haircut," said Cherry Sue.

Poppleton looked at his three dear friends.
Such good friends.
"And I can take you all out for ice cream!"
said Poppleton.

Which he did.

On their way back home, Poppleton traded the wallpaper for some paint.

His friends were the finest painters
in town.